MOM, ARE YOU THERE?

RAINBOW ABEGG

Cover image by © Photodisc Green/Getty Images.

Interior images from: *Spot Illustrations from Women's Magazines of the Teens and Twenties, 2001 Decorative Cuts and Ornaments, Treasury of Art Nouveau Design & Ornament, Art Nouveau Motifs and Vignettes, Pictorial Archive of Printer's Ornaments from the Renaissance to the 20th Century, Children and their World: A Treasury of Vintage Cuts and Illustrations, Vintage Spot Illustrations of Children: 795 Cuts from the Teens and Twenties, Children: A Pictorial Archive of Permission-Free Illustrations,* © Dover Publications.

Cover design copyrighted 2004 by Covenant Communications, Inc.

Published by Covenant Communications, Inc.
American Fork, Utah

Printed in Canada
First Printing: March 2004

11 10 09 08 07 06 05 04   10 9 8 7 6 5 4 3 2 1

ISBN 1-59156-437-9

For mothers everywhere

who guide their children to look

heavenward. Also, for my mother

Jana McKnight

and my mother-in-law Olie Abegg.

When I was
born, my mom planted a lilac bush. She loved
the fragrance of lilacs and she said
I was the sweetest-smelling baby ever.

**M**y mom
was always planting something.
Before I could crawl, she would set me on a blanket
next to her while she dug in the garden.
Then she would sing to me:

I'll be the gardener.

You be the vine.

Let's reach up to heaven

By harvest time.

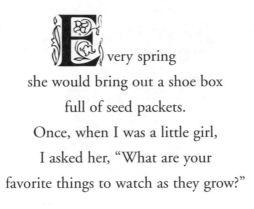

very spring
she would bring out a shoe box
full of seed packets.
Once, when I was a little girl,
I asked her, "What are your
favorite things to watch as they grow?"

"**K**ids,"
she replied as she
pulled on my braid.

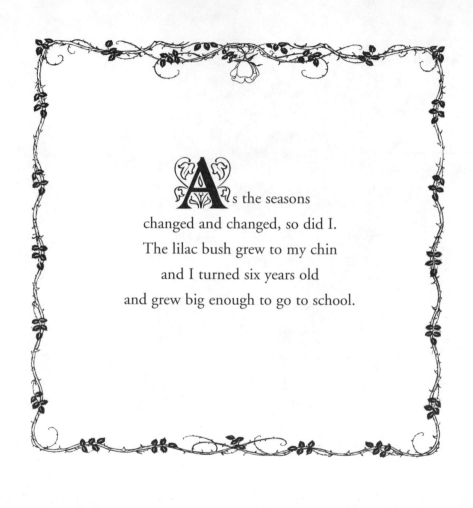

As the seasons
changed and changed, so did I.
The lilac bush grew to my chin
and I turned six years old
and grew big enough to go to school.

My mom liked to have cookies waiting for me when I came home. Even if they were store bought, they sure did taste good. One afternoon when I came home, the house was very quiet. "Mom, are you there?" I yelled.

I heard her voice echo, "I'm up here." In the hallway I saw the hanging stairs pulled down from the attic.

Poking her dirt-smudged face out
of the attic doorway, she smiled down at me.
"What are you doing up there?" I asked.

Going through
my memories, living in the past,
thinking, crying, laughing, and remembering,"
she answered.
"Come on up. You can be my guest
as we travel back in time."

e stayed up there for hours looking through all kinds of stuff. Mom dusted off an old scrapbook and we looked through it page by page. I ran my fingers over a lacy valentine she had made in the third grade.

Opening an old trunk,
Mom pulled out a folded stack of baby clothes
she had saved since I was a newborn.
I stared at my little white blessing dress.
I couldn't believe I had ever fit into such a tiny thing.
She touched the delicate dress and smelled it,
then she hugged me.

ext, we tried on funny old hats. There was a black one with netting that covered my face. "That would be good to keep the mosquitoes out while we're in the mountains," I said. She grinned.

"Grandma wore it to her cousin's funeral."

"Were there mosquitoes there?"

Mom just laughed.

As the seasons changed and changed, so did I. Purple clusters of flowers burst out on the lilac bush. When I turned thirteen, Mom said that I'd blossomed too. In junior high, Doug Hunter passed a note to me. I could hardly breathe. I had a crush on him. After school I ran home to tell my mom. The front door was locked, so I ran around the house to the back door. I stuck my head inside and yelled, "Mom, are you there?"

Her muffled voice answered,
"I'm up here." I backed up a few steps to see
her on the roof. Waving the note, I told her
about Doug. She smiled down at me.
"What are you doing up there?" I asked.

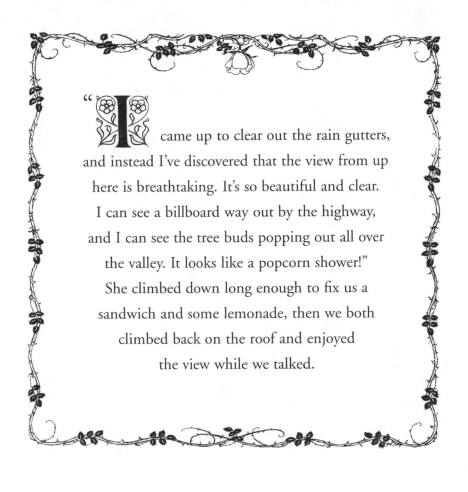

"I came up to clear out the rain gutters, and instead I've discovered that the view from up here is breathtaking. It's so beautiful and clear. I can see a billboard way out by the highway, and I can see the tree buds popping out all over the valley. It looks like a popcorn shower!" She climbed down long enough to fix us a sandwich and some lemonade, then we both climbed back on the roof and enjoyed the view while we talked.

As the seasons changed and changed, so did I. One year, when I came home from college for the summer, I noticed the lilac bush had grown tall and was branching out. It looked so independent. Then, on a holiday weekend, my family went camping. Mom woke up early while it was still dark. Pretty soon, I could smell the bacon cooking, so I got up too. The pan was simmering over the fire, but I couldn't see her anywhere.

hen I spotted her on a narrow path, hiking through an area with steep, rocky walls. I followed, but I couldn't catch her. It was as if she disappeared into thin air.

A little scared, I called softly, "Mom, are you there?"

She stuck her head over the cliff above me, whispering, "I'm up here. Don't worry, I'll help you up the path." Then she came down, took my hand, and showed me the way up to the ledge. She patted a place beside her on a rock, and I sat down.

"What are you doing up here?" I asked.

"**E**njoying Heavenly Father's creations and watching the world give birth to a brand-new day," she answered.

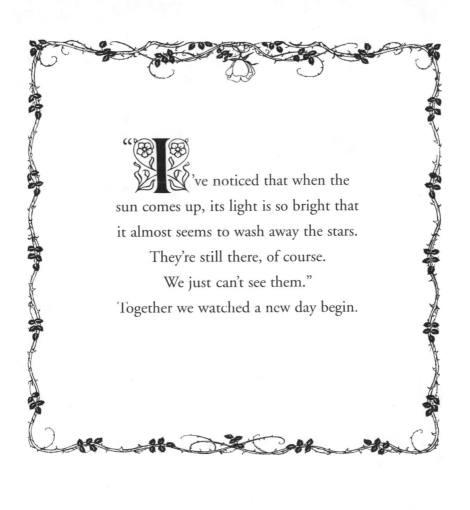

"I've noticed that when the sun comes up, its light is so bright that it almost seems to wash away the stars.

They're still there, of course.

We just can't see them."

Together we watched a new day begin.

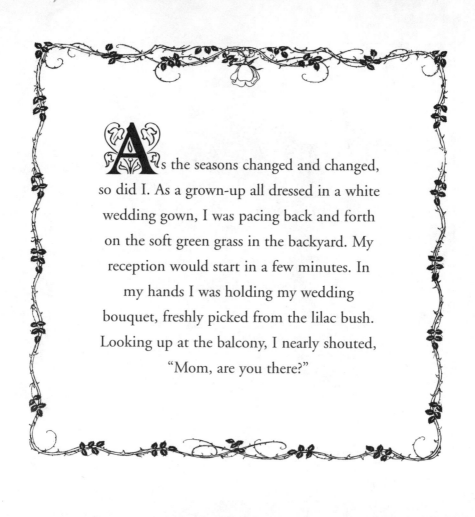

As the seasons changed and changed, so did I. As a grown-up all dressed in a white wedding gown, I was pacing back and forth on the soft green grass in the backyard. My reception would start in a few minutes. In my hands I was holding my wedding bouquet, freshly picked from the lilac bush. Looking up at the balcony, I nearly shouted, "Mom, are you there?"

She stepped out to the metal railing with a worried look on her face. "I'm up here," she called back. "I just talked to the caterer. They made a mistake. They thought your wedding was *next* Saturday."

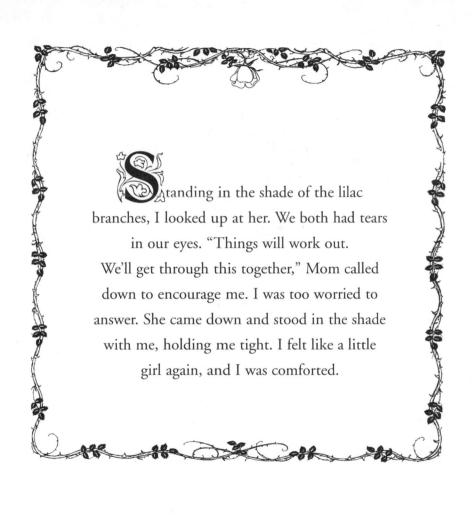

Standing in the shade of the lilac branches, I looked up at her. We both had tears in our eyes. "Things will work out. We'll get through this together," Mom called down to encourage me. I was too worried to answer. She came down and stood in the shade with me, holding me tight. I felt like a little girl again, and I was comforted.

My uncle made a fizzy drink from soda pop and lemonade. We served it from the crystal punch bowl, along with a big silver tray filled with pretzels and popcorn. I looked at Mom again as the guests began to arrive. She shrugged, and we both burst out laughing. Mom said my wedding would be remembered for years. And it was.

As the seasons changed and changed, so did my mom. She grew older, and weaker, and became very sick. The old lilac bush was heavy with blossoms, and the last time I saw Mom, I brought her an armful of them. She tried to smile and whispered:

I'LL BE THE GARDENER.

YOU BE THE VINE.

LET'S REACH UP TO HEAVEN

BY HARVEST TIME.

om knew it was her time to go back to Heavenly Father. She said she could garden there all year long, because in heaven everything is always in bloom.

But it was hard to have her go. Somehow I know that the hurt I still feel is a gift; hurting means I lost something precious. Missing her now means that I knew she was always there for me—she mattered in my life. Needing her means she gave me so much, and a child *never* stops needing a mom. She planted so many good seeds in my heart. I will miss her always.

As the seasons changed and changed,
so did I. Wandering in my mom's backyard,
I found a tiny lilac bush growing by the big old lilac
bush my mother had planted. I dug it up and
planted it in my own backyard. Dusting the dirt off
my hands, I watched the sun slowly sink,
and I sighed as little stars began poking out in the
dark blue sky. I called out softly,
"Mom, are you there?"

It wasn't cold outside, but I got goose bumps. I'm not sure if I heard it or felt it, but it was almost Mom's voice saying, "I'm up here."

"What are you doing up there?" I asked quietly.

I felt like a little girl again,
safe in her arms, and I was comforted.
I stood on the porch and stared up at the heavens.
From somewhere the scent of lilacs floated in
the breeze. I thought about my mom.
I know she's up there. Then, from behind me,
I heard the quiet steps of my own little girl.

"**W**hat are you
doing up there?"
I asked quietly.

A whisper answered, "Going through my memories, living in the past, thinking, crying, laughing, and remembering. The view from up here is breathtaking. It's so beautiful and clear.

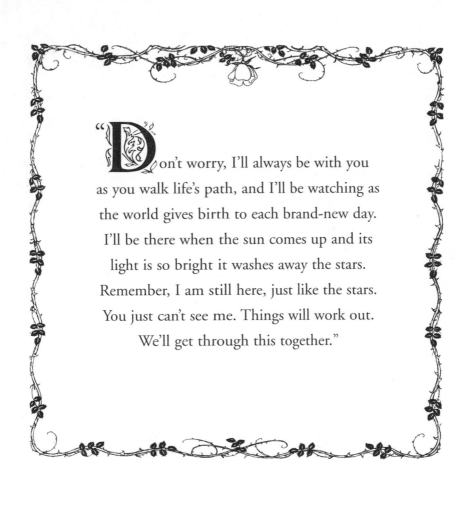

"Don't worry, I'll always be with you as you walk life's path, and I'll be watching as the world gives birth to each brand-new day. I'll be there when the sun comes up and its light is so bright it washes away the stars. Remember, I am still here, just like the stars. You just can't see me. Things will work out. We'll get through this together."

I felt like a little girl again,
safe in her arms, and I was comforted.
I stood on the porch and stared up at the heavens.
From somewhere the scent of lilacs floated in
the breeze. I thought about my mom.
I know she's up there. Then, from behind me,
I heard the quiet steps of my own little girl.

"**M**om, are you there?"

"I'm right here," I said. She came and snuggled in my arms and I whispered in her ear, "I'll always be right here. Did I ever tell you about the song my mom used to sing to me?"

I'LL BE THE GARDENER,
YOU BE THE VINE . . .

I could feel Mom smile.